Dear Reader,

This sexy bundle was created especially for the author's fans. Her readers are her inspiration and keep her going. Without you there wouldn't be any Paranormal stories as kinky as these!

Seduced by Bigfoot

and Ravaged by the Yeti

The Secret Adventures of a Fertile Housewife

By Eva Roche-Poésy

Chapter 1: Betty Homemaker

Betty Bedford was a typical small-town housewife in rural Vermont. Devoted, loving; she pressed the sheets, bleached the doilies, folded the laundry, styled her hair, packed her husband's lunch and dutifully made love to said hardworking husband each night. Mr. Bradford was no stallion in bed, nor was he prudent - he was simply easy to please. They met in bed at 10:00 each night. When Brad shut off his reading light, that was her cue to close her book and accept him. He would reach over, caress her shoulder and then mount her. Foreplay was nil, for he found it tedious. He entered her by way of missionary position and mechanically thrust himself in and out of her, while she paid extra care to keep her hair in place. Betty took pride in her hair, as vain as it made her feel - and vanity was looked down upon where she was from - but her soft, luscious locks made her smile when she looked in the mirror. Mr. Bradford complimented her hair when it was shiny and smooth.

Making love to Brad was a nice routine for Betty - she gained no satisfaction from it, but her hopes of creating life kept her optimistic. Brad made love for six minutes each time and afterwards dismounted her, apologizing, "Sorry, honey, I'll make it up to you tomorrow. I've had such a long day and I'm really tired." Brad was asleep by the time he finished his sentence. Betty would wait a few more minutes for Brad to fall into a deeper slumber. Like a feather, she floated across the floor into the bathroom, drew the curtains and opened the window. She reached up between the storm window and screen for her packet of cigarettes. Brad didn't know his wife smoked - and he wouldn't like it if he found out - but this was her release - a gift to herself, to have a silent moment to gaze at the stars twinkling in the night sky. As her mouth made a wide "O" the smoke drifted out; her mind drifted with nary a thought in her head. Curiously, on this particular night she felt she was being watched. Betty Squinted her eyes and peered into the dark woods beyond their home. She was sure she saw a shadowy figure flicker in the moonlight.

Chapter 2: Betty Baker

The alarm rang at 6:05 and by 7:30am Brad Bradford had gulped the remains of his coffee, slipped on his Spring trench coat and was out door, "Bye, hun, see you at dinner." Betty didn't know it, but that would be the last time she saw Brad. She loosened the belt of her robe, for the time Brad is not home is the time she is free! *Alone is more like it,* she sighed, mulling over all the endless chores and errands to run. She decided to start her day with a task she enjoyed: she would bake a couple pies! It was a sunny day and she had a basketful of fresh strawberries purchased from the farmers market the day before. Brad loved her Strawberry pie. *Everyone* loved Betty's pies. Betty lowered her hand and rested it on her tight belly. She felt the warmth of her flesh radiating on her hand. After three years of trying for a baby she was beginning to feel hopeless. Brad finished inside her every night, though to no success. Betty imagined when she made her pies she was baking with love for her children; little feet pattering around the house, tugging on her apron, impatiently watching the pies cool on the window sill with big, puppy dog eyes. She wanted to be a mother. She *needed* to be a mother. Betty sighed and decided she would donate the second pie to the church. *Someday I'm going to get tired of being little old me,* she assured herself, tying the ribbons of her polka dotted apron.

A cozy, sugary-sweet aroma wafted throughout her home as she began to hum. The first pie was nearly done baking when she began the second. She tossed a little flour onto her board like an expert baker and began patting a ball of dough. As she was about to roll out the crust, a dark figure quickly blocked the sun from filtering through the window, and as soon as it appeared it was gone again. Startled, Betty knocked over the rest of her sugar with the rolling pin, *"Oh, horsefeathers!"* She cursed. "Well, that was the last of it. I'll go ask Mrs Merryweather if I can borrow a cup from her."

She dusted her hands upon her apron and headed out the door. Sauntering down the walkway was one of her neighbor's black cats. It had a small white spot on its nose, like a permanent snowflake. *Must have been you.*

"Mrew?," the cat asked, tilting its head.

Betty stepped off her pathway and crossed the perfectly trimmed green grass to the neighbor's home and knocked against the door's wooden frame.

"Good morning, Mrs. Merryweather," "Good morning, dear," replied a petite figure, peering out from the screen door.

"I'm sorry to bother you so early. I started making a pie for the church, but my butterfingers dropped the last bit of sugar. May I please borrow a cup from you?"

"Of course, dear, come in. Excuse the mess, Wendy is such a tornado." Wendy is Mrs. Merryweather's home aide. She also works hard to keep her home clean, which isn't her job. Her home was spotless and everything had been in its place since the day Mr. Merryweather passed away. Betty admired her clean home and wondered if Wendy had been doing all the cleaning what did Mrs. Merryweather do with all her time, without a man that needed tending to?

"Here you are, dear."

"You are very kind, Mrs. Merryweather. Bye, now."

"My pleasure, dear. See you on Sunday?"

"Yes, Mrs. Merryweather, see you on Sunday." Betty cringed as the regretful words escaped her mouth and felt the light in her heart dim. She was aware that Sunday's were the Lord's day, but Betty was aching to get out of her small town and go on a long drive with her husband. She had the *naughtiest* idea: to get away from their small town, drive fast and feel the wind in her hair - and make love in a motel. She thought that was dirty and it made her smile.

As Betty perched her foot on the first step of her front porch, she paused; she felt watched. She looked around, but didn't see anyone. *Oh, it's probably old Mr. Calhoun - that peeping tom!* She glanced at his home, but didn't see any rustling by the curtains. She still felt eyes on her and it made her nervous. Betty slipped quickly inside and shut the door. And then locked it. *Just room for the Lord in here.*

Betty arrived in the kitchen and saw her strawberry pie resting on the windowsill. The fragrant room was delicious, but she was sure she left it in the oven. *Silly me I haven't had my coffee yet. I must have taken it out. It would have burned anyhow.* She thanked the man above for watching out for her - at least *someone* was watching out for her. Betty glided across the kitchen to the windowsill. The pie beckoned her to smell it closely and inhale the fragrant berries and sweet, caramelized sugar, butter and vanilla. She inhaled deeply, filling her senses with pleasure. Saliva gathered in her mouth and just as she was about to swallow, something dashed behind the tree.

Betty's heart stopped. *Did I just imagine that?* A large figure - *very* large - stepped out from behind a tree and glared at her. "What in God's green... Is that a man?" Betty was beside herself with curiosity. *That's a very large… and hairy - oh, my, that is a beast!*

Betty spun around and pinned her back to the wall. Her heart was pounding out of her chest.

What does it want? My pie, surely it's after my sweet pie. Perhaps if I offer my pie to him, he will leave and go back to where he came from.

Betty peered around the corner and out the window: the tall, dark, hairy figure stood there, still as a stone with his dark, coal eyes serious and impatient.

Chapter 2: Bigfoot

 The ominous figure watched as she hesitantly approached it. His dark, emotionless face watched her every move. Her pie rattled in the foil as her trembling fingers did their best not to flee.

She made it halfway across the yard and stopped

before the big oak trees. She bent down to leave the pie before him, but didn't notice that her robe had opened slightly, revealing her soft, tender cleavage. Bigfoot liked it and beckoned her closer with a draw of his large, thick finger. She lifted the pie from the soft blades of grass. Step by step she grew closer to him; each step she saw in more detail who this large ominous figure was: standing at least 9' tall, this thick-bodied and muscular creature boasted broad shoulders, powerful tree trunk legs and thick, dark hair that covered him like body armor. Even his feet were enormous. *This is no human*. His dark liquid eyes glared at her. *This is no beast*.

Not three feet away from him, she could smell his existence, his natural musk, like earth and wood. His hormones, though she couldn't detect them, drew her in closer. *What is this creature? I have heard of Bigfoot and Yetis before, but I thought those were mythical creatures. Surely, God wouldn't have put such sinful creatures on our planet. I heard they kidnap people and commit adultery; rough and brutal acts.* She raised her shaking arms and offered her olive branch. *Perhaps, since he is only after my pie he will take it and leave.* The strawberry pie tempted Bigfoots senses (strawberries are regarded a delicious and highly sought-after treat in the forest). Here was a treat with a delicious scent wafting over to him; the sugary aroma made him salivate, but it was when it swirled with the scent of this innocent, clean and dainty human, this delicate flower of a human - a *fertile woman* - is when it became intoxicating. His sense of smell was much keener than a dog's, and his primal instinct more powerful, therefore he could smell how fertile she was. Her young, supple body was ovulating and releasing pheromones so strong he could taste them. Her body was *begging* to be fertilized; it was time Bigfoot claimed his mate.

Chapter 3: Ravaged by Nature

Her eyes were wide and her heart throbbed inside her chest as she held the pie with outstretched arms. His large, leathery hands resembled baseball gloves with thick tufts of hair and reached towards her; the enormous sausage-link fingers unfolded. Betty placed the tiny pie into his calloused palm without taking her eyes off his. She blinked - unsure if this were really happening . Bigfoot's large hand wrapped around Betty's waist and drew her towards him. He cupped her buttocks and lifted her to his chest. Like a child, she peered over his shoulder and pondered the great depths of the forest and what would come of her. Her heart pounded, though she didn't feel afraid. There was a sense of relief as she saw her little white house and perfectly manicured lawn disappear beyond the big oak trees as Bigfoot stomped into the forest. Betty fit perfectly in the palm of his hand. *What will come of me? Will I see Brad again? Will I ever make it back home?* Betty watched the last patches of white disappear behind the trees as they ventured deeper into the forest. *Was it home?*

Bigfoot stomped for hours through the forest, into the mountains, over boulders; he yanked down vines and knocked down trees that got in his way. They came upon a clearing on the side of a mountain, with even ground and an entrance to a small cave, which she deemed must be his home (though it was the middle of nowhere to Betty). The sun was at its highest point and beat down warmly on her exposed shoulder. He placed her down on a mossy spot by a tree with a *thud*.

"Well, that's not very nice." Betty folded her arms and shot Bigfoot a look.

"Grumpf." *Bigfoot* was not a master of communication - especially with women, but the few encounters he had - a Yeti who lived higher up in the mountains - and with nature itself, was simply through a few grunts of varying pitch. He was not interested in conversation anyhow, for his sole purpose of taking this human was his inner drive to mate. She was tiny, but there were no female Bigfeet, and he had smelled her pie from miles away.

"Oh dear, you're bleeding," Betty noticed a thin trail of blood running down Bigfoot's trunk of a leg, the thick tufts of hair directing the trail every-which-way. "A thorn must have caught you. Here," Betty tore a tiny square from the hem of her satin robe and perched onto her knees to wipe the blood.

"*Grumpf*!" Bigfoot thrust Betty backwards with his foot and slammed her against the tree behind her. The satin square dabbed with blood flew from her hand.

"You brute!" She yelled up at him, exasperated by his terrible manners, "don't you treat me like that! I only -"

Bigfoot took a large thick rope from behind a boulder and dropped one end across her legs; he slowly circled the tree, stomping the ground with his enormous feet. Betty could feel the ground shake each time the massive creature shifted his weight with a *thud, thud, thud.*

"I only wanted to help you. You don't have to tie me up. Please don't." Betty tried to push the possibility of being his *food* and not *friend* out of her head.

Her fairly large bosoms were strangled between two rounds of rope and her robe had fallen from both shoulders. Betty felt helpless - she *was* helpless, but she found some comfort in the fact that her mundane life had taken an unexpected turn. It was exhilarating to have her life in the hands of this enormous man-beast. *What does he want with me?* He knotted the rope a few times.

"I don't think that makes much of a

difference," Betty reasoned, "I'm no good alone in a forest and we're hours away from civilization. I won't run, I promise."

"Grumpf!" He tightened the last knot.

Bigfoot stood up to admire his prize. *This human is mine.* From head to toe he observed his slave-mate, whose sole purpose now was to be his vessel for offspring, or - if he preferred - his food. Her soft chestnut hair fell in large bouncing curls over the generous mounds of her chest. He admired how her bosoms were strangled between the rope; the pressure of fabric stretching thin over her bosoms.

He peeled the foil pan away from the pie and held it in one hand. For Bigfoot, the pie was the size of a cookie. He took a bite of the sweet dessert, which was more than half of the entire pie, and watched his slave nervously shift beneath the rope. A rock was poking the underside of her thigh and she lifted her knee in hopes of relieving the piercing pressure, but her movement slipped the satin robe open and off her thighs. His eyes were drawn to a small dark patch of hair. He took another enormous bite of her pie; the contrast of the sweet sugar and tart berries danced on his tongue. Bigfoot was still hungry and could smell that Betty kept an even sweeter treat - her *own* pie - hidden between her thighs. Bigfoot's groin started to tingle.

Chapter 4: The Monster

He approached Betty, his female human-slave, and presented his member, which was growing steadily in length and girth, while his breath grew heavy. Unsure of her fate, she studied his movements as he towered closer; at that moment her jaw fell - mouth agape, as she noticed what was hanging there between his legs - *and growing!* She couldn't take her eyes off it. She couldn't close her mouth, because she was so shocked and in awe of its size. The gargantuan member swayed in front of her face, it was longer than her forearm and thicker than a soda can. Bigfoot was pleased at her reaction and stood proudly as it grew longer, thicker, and started to rise towards her. It seemed to be reaching for her. She calculated it to be about the length of her arm now and the thickness - she just couldn't comprehend it. The biggest (and only) penis she had seen before was her husband's - a fair 6" on a good day and her thumb and forefinger easily slipped around the shaft. But this one-eyed monster stared at her, expectantly. Her mouth still agape, she looked up into his eyes as if to plead with him - it wasn't the sinful act of cheating that worried her, in fact it never entered her mind - it was that she couldn't fathom that massive *limb* entering her tiny body.

He towered over her; his hairy, muscular chest heaved with each breath as he glared down at her, his mouth salivating. An enormous hairy foot with thick, yellow nails and tufts of hair on each toe stomped to the left side of her - and then another landed at her right. The one-eyed monster wavered in the air and hung down in front of her nose. With her arms tied tightly to her sides she knew she was in no position to refuse. It lingered there staring at her; the monster's long hairy shaft was filling with blood as the veins protruded, pulsating. She could feel it's warmth radiating from its bulbous tip.

"*Grumpf*!"

Betty was startled by his sudden grunt, for she was quite mesmerized by what stared back at her.

"There's nothing small about Bigfoot is there?" Betty joked. *Maybe he has a sense of humor.*

The behemoth of a sexual organ extended out from its foreskin and presented its large, bulbous red glans.

What does he expect me to do with this thing? It would be like trying to suck off my own thigh! This better be worth not being eaten alive.

She leant her head towards him and brushed her

soft cheek against his massive member. She felt the weight of it knock against her head as it bounced upwards in response to her touch. She had excited it. She looked up at the huge man-beast and into his eyes; he glared at her and -

"*Grumpf!*" She received a good whack from the cock to the side of her head, ordering her to continue. She stretched her neck out as far as she could and caressed her lips and nose along his veiny shaft all the way down to the hot, sensitive tip. Tentatively, she gave it a soft lick, like she would to a melting scoop of her favorite ice cream. Betty savored the taste; it was unlike her husbands, which was tangy and a little acerbic. The man-beasts fleshy glans tasted much like an earthier combination of honey, seawater and wildflower. It was a very surprising - and welcoming - taste from such an unexpected creature. She licked her favorite ice cream again and again and caressed her face against the slippery wet tip.

"*Grrrrm...*"

Oh, I do hope he is enjoying this. I would much rather stay alive, and as dirty as this is I quite enjoy the challenge. Betty studied the gaping hole of his enormous glans, and stuck her small tongue into it. She began drawing large circles, tickling its tender, salty inside, but it began dancing and jumping into the air and hitting her face. *This is no good, I won't be able to please him without holding that thing down.* Little did Betty know, but Bigfoot did not have a harem of women pleasing him, nor did he yet master manual stimulation. Days when he was too pent up he would resolve it by rubbing himself against a tree. Today was one of those days, especially because of Betty's incredible scent and pheromones driving him mad. He slapped his hard cock against her face a few times as she tried to lick his swollen glans in passing; veins protruded from his hairy shaft as it pulsed and pulsed. Another smack of his throbbing bulbous tip against her head was enough to send his testicles into his body and with forceful, spastic contractions, semen pulsed through his shaft as he ejaculated; hot, thick semen gushed into her face and on her body, spewing with each contraction.

"*Grrrruuuuaaaahhhh!*"

 Betty was dripping in steaming, salty cum. She opened her mouth in hopes of getting air. As his semen dripped down into her mouth, she reflected on all the times Brad had came inside her, into her mouth and onto her belly. This one ejaculation was more cum she had ever experienced in her entire life

- and it came from the biggest cock she had ever seen.

Bigfoot watched proudly as his semen drenched his slave. It matted her hair, covered her entire face like thick cream, poured down onto her breasts and all over her body. Bigfoot's scrotum was still convulsing as his softening cock squeezed out the remains of what had so long been stored inside him.

Betty did not expect Bigfoot to be a creature of romance, but she was appalled as she watched him walk away, leaving her tied to the tree, and into his cave.

"Hey!" She called after him, "Why don't you untie me! That *brute*."

Moments later, Bigfoot reappeared, dragging a dead

deer behind him.

"Hey," she called again, "Please don't leave me like this - I'm so cold! Please untie me. I won't run."

Bigfoot ignored his slave as he stomped around his clearing collecting branches and twigs. He piled the wood in his usual spot and began rubbing two dry sticks together under the warm rays of the midday sun - and a little help from foraged broken glass.

"I can help you build a fire. I was a Girl Scout."

Bigfoot's efforts were beginning to show true when small puffs of smoke emerged from beneath his hands. He stood before his strong, tumbling fire and threw the deer upon it.

"Oh, well, that's not very efficient." Betty condemned him for his waste. Bigfoot sat on the other side of the fire, with his back towards Betty. He didn't like all the noise this human made.

"*Men.*" Betty sighed. She thought about home and wondered if Brad was back already. She wondered if he was looking for her or looking for dinner. Her thoughts were disturbed by a loud *crack*, *grind* and then a juicy tearing of the deer's hind leg. Bigfoot's primal needs were temporarily satiated. Gnawing cartilage from the bone, he rose to his feet and stomped over to his prisoner. He dropped a chunk of flesh and muscle matted with bits of charred fur next to her thigh.

"My hands are tied," Betty grumbled.

 Bigfoot turned around and headed towards his cave.

"Hey, hey, wait! Please don't leave me like this!" She

called, hopelessly.

Chapter 5: Rapture

The morning sun peeked over the horizon with soft rays that seemed to kiss the treetops before her. Dew drops on flowers and foliage around her sparkled like tiny diamonds. Betty awoke with a stiff neck, still tied to the tree and chilly, but she sensed today was the day she started living. The summer air quickly warmed with the rising sun.

She thought she was alone until she heard a few footsteps crunching and breaking sticks along the way. Bigfoot approached Betty's mossy spot and, with unnatural ease, pushed the tree, breaking it free from its roots and slipped her out from of the coiled rope. He picked up his trusty spear and hoisted her crusty body down the mountain until they came to a stream, in which he tossed her. She balanced herself on the uneven rocks and pebbles and combed her slender fingers through the cool clean water. She cleansed her face. She rinsed the slime from her hair and dabbed water on her neck. Bigfoot tugged at her robe and pulled it off her. Naked and exposed, she obeyed him and poured water over her body with cupped hands as he watched. She had almost cleansed herself of all the caked on sperm, when Bigfoot decided he had enough watching and needed some doing. He grabbed his mate and forced her over a tree stump. Her naked, wet body experienced pain as the loose shards of wood clung to her; the jagged tree stump burned her sensitive breasts as he manhandled her from behind. Bigfoot kicked her tiny feet to the sides of the stump and stood between her legs. He pressed his rough palms on her lush ass and spread her cheeks apart; his already erect cock rubbed against her pussy. Her velvety pussy and silky hair tickled his shaft and sent all the blood in his body pulsing into his throbbing cock. He lifted his massive monster and rubbed the head against her pussy lips; the precum seeping out from his cock making them slippery and wet. He began thrusting his giant bulbous tip into her tiny pussy; working it slowly deeper inside her. Betty was astounded both at the sheer volume she was feeling inside her and at this incredibly dirty act. *Release me* she beckoned inside herself, *release me you filthy animal!* Bigfoot could only fit the head of his throbbing cock into her sopping pussy as he began to feel the overwhelming and unstoppable climax he so deliciously wanted; he took her there, with claws deeply embedded in her body, he claimed her as his as he thrust forth and spewed his seed deep within her; each contraction ejecting more and more steaming cum into her body as he filled every crevice with his sperm.

"Oh, my God! Oh!" Her pussy cavity could not handle the volume of his cum and was expelled with each ejection of steaming sperm. His juice oozed out of her, dripping to the floor and blanketing her legs.

Bigfoot thrust his spear into the stream and stabbed a long, feisty trout. The branch passed through the middle of its body, but it fought long and hard, flipping its tail and trying to wriggle itself off the spear before finally going limp.

Bigfoot tossed Betty a leather satchel, which hit her

chest and fell to the floor. She picked it up and turning it over, shrugged, "Yes? A bag - what do you need?"

"Grumpf!" He pointed to a row of bushes. "*Argrumpf*!" He growled again, pointing with his spear.

Betty hustled over to the bushes and realized what he meant - *Ahh, these are blueberry bushes! Ok, I shall collect them.*

During her loyal picking, Betty also gathered raspberries, blackberries, acorns, hazelnuts, wild herbs, dandelions and stones she found beautiful.

They went back to the camp to eat, which was to be berries and fish. As Bigfoot set out to gather dry sticks and kindling, Betty scurried over to her leather sack and laid out the surprises she found down by the stream. She began by grinding the nuts and herbs into a fragrant mixture and rubbed it inside the fish's belly. Bigfoot wasn't impressed and snatched the trout from her hands. He was about to throw it into the fire, just as he did with the deer, but Betty ran in front of him, waving the spear in desperation.

"No, no, wait! Please let me cook the fish, you will love it!" She stabbed the spear through the overlapped skin of the fish, thus closing the gaping hole where she had stuffed the nuts and herbs. The fish's skin started to sizzle and pop over the fire. It emitted a deliciously cozy smell, which warmed Betty to the core. Her expert eyes knew the inside was beginning to flake so she pulled the fish from the fire. As Betty was just about to slide the perfectly cooked fish from the spear, Bigfoot snatched it from her hands up and chomped half of it off; its head and skeleton crunching between his teeth. Betty shivered as she reflected on the man-beast's true power and how he can simply fling her off the cliff to her doom, should the urge present itself. Betty's slender fingers plucked warm chunks of fresh trout from its carcass and idly fed herself as she stared into the crackling fire.

Bigfoot scraped a thick fingernail at the bark of a tree and lapped as the sap oozed out. It was Bigfoot's coveted maple tree. He gathered some sap on a sturdy leaf and made love to the sticky goodness with his tongue. A tiny light of hope flickered deep within Betty's heart. She had an idea.

Chapter 6: Betty does Yeti

The next morning, Betty snuck away from Bigfoot's camp before the the first sliver of rose-colored sunlight peeked over the horizon. (Apparently, there *was* something small about Bigfoot: his brain. He had tied Betty to the broken tree's stump the night before, but when he retreated to his cave she simply slipped the coiled rope over the stump and slept peacefully on the mossy floor). She headed down the mountain towards the clearing where she had found so many nuts and berries the day before. When she reached the stream, she foraged for as many nuts and berries as she could and used her robe as a makeshift sack. Naked and vulnerable, she scurried back up the mountain. Betty worked diligently grinding away at the nuts; she would not be pleased until it was a uniform texture. Utilizing the naturally occurring oils, she molded the nut paste firmly together with dandelion leaves into the shape of a tart shell. She heated the wild strawberries and forest berries inside of a soda can, which she perched on the glowing embers from last night's fire. This helped the natural sugars in the berries to meld together and become even more fragrant. She scuttled over to Bigfoot's beloved maple tree and scraped at the same spot with a stick. When the sap started to flow, she gathered as much as she could into the berry mixture, stirring gently with a twig. As the delicious aroma started to tickle her nose, she heard a rustle from behind her. Betty realized the sun had already began to peek over the horizon, which meant Bigfoot would be up any moment - she had to hurry!

Bigfoot stomped out from his abode groggily. Angry and bewildered, he spun around, *Why is slave not tied tree!* A warm, sugary aroma tickled his nose and distracted him, *What smell?* He saw his human-slave checking over her tart's state of perfection: the gooey berries dripping with sweet sap on a plate of dandelion leaves looked incredible. She smiled coyly at Bigfoot and batted her lush lashes over her large, childish eyes and proudly handed over the tart.

"Good morning sl--"

He slapped the tart from Betty's hand and it rolled across the ground, collecting every dead leaf it touched.

"Grumpf!"

How dare human defile Bigfoot camp and use Bigfoot tools and Bigfoot sugar tree! How dare slave leave! Betty was overwhelmed with sadness and anger. Memories of being scolded as a little girl by her military father haunted her. She thought for sure this would earn her some lashings and she dropped her head into her hands and began to cry.

Crunch. Stomp.

Bigfoot's ears perked up as Betty peeked through her wet fingers. They felt eyes on them; lurking, calculating eyes. Someone - *something* was making its way down the mountain and it didn't sound small. Bigfoot started to grunt.

"Grumpf! Grumpf-grumpf!" He was urging her and pointing, but she couldn't see details through her tears. If it was someone from her town coming to rescue her, then she didn't care. She felt silly and ashamed of the feelings and curiosity she had built around that *beast*. She felt hopeless and realized it was time to face the fact that with Brad is where she belonged. She should never have left home, shouldn't have given her pie away - he's ungrateful

and doesn't deserve it! At that moment the tentative footsteps became quick, crackling stomps that sent sticks, leaves and small animals scattering in every direction. Betty wiped her eyes and struggled to focused through the puffy lids, "What in the world is - *another* beast?!"

Slinging himself down the mountain from tree trunk to tree trunk at an incredible speed, the beast landed on Bigfoot's clearing with a *boom*. He was massive. Bigfoot picked up his spear without taking his eyes from the intruder. The great white beast stood up tall, unfurling his fingers and toes as he grounded himself in the enemy's soil. He was bigger than Bigfoot.

Was he related to Bigfoot? Betty wondered. He was a funny looking man-beast with long thick tufts of white, wiry hair jutting out from his cheeks and ears.

Betty found him a bit comical with his permanent grimace and snow white caterpillar monobrow. *Since the beast traveled all the way down from the snow capped mountains he must be a yeti! What good did school ever do for me when they lie about these great beasts being merely mythical creatures?* Bigfoot stepped in front of Betty and glared at the Yeti. They stared at each other; no one dared to move. Betty wondered if he, too, had smelled the berries simmering over the embers.

"*Arhuugh*!" The yeti announced himself into the sky like a howling wolf. He had a higher toned grunt, but undoubtedly more powerful. He boasted broad shoulders and a thick barrel waist, virtually no neck, hair poured out from his ears and his pale, weathered skin sagged like a tired old sack. He looked older than Bigfoot and not necessarily wiser, but he most certainly wanted *something* .

"*Grumpf*!" Bigfoot stomped his foot on the ground.

"*Arhuugh*!" Insisted the Yeti and beat twice on his belly.

"*Grumpf*!" This time Bigfoot's argument was carried by a snarl. Betty became worried, she could feel the tension between these two rising. *Perhaps they have fought over a woman before? Perhaps he wanted me as food?*

 The yeti lurched towards Bigfoot, sending branches and leaves flurrying into the air, Bigfoot stood strong with his spear and anticipated a strong hit from the yeti; the yeti pounded the ground with his white, furry feet as the two beasts wrestled and struggled force against force; an almost even battle, the yeti standing a full foot taller than Bigfoot, but Bigfoot was younger and more agile. The sun beat strongly on the two warriors as they pushed and pulled sending logs, rocks leaves and bones from previous meals soaring over the cliff. Betty retreated to the cave and worried, twisting the cloth of her robe in angst. Bigfoot gave the yeti a solid whack on the head with his great wooden spear, which in turn infuriated the yeti. He charged towards Bigfoot like a linebacker and rammed his stomach with his broad shoulders, knocking the wind out of him. The yeti then crouched down and lifted him up off the ground and threw Bigfoot with all his might, sending him toppling over the cliff. Betty's stomach flipped as she saw the beast she regarded her savior, her protector, flail helplessly over the edge, she heard branches and earth suffering beneath him with each crack, *crash* and *thud* down the mountain. The yeti wasted no time and didn't bother watching his foe -

his competition - suffer.

The yeti pounded his feet upon the ground as he turned towards Betty. Snorting and huffing with adrenaline and exertion, he slowly stomped his way towards his cowering prize. She shuffled her knees backwards into the cave. She regretted not having taken the opportunity to properly hide, for her curiosity got the best of her. She had seen before and knew the art of sumo wrestling, but what she had just witnessed was far more thrilling, far more exhilarating and titillating. The yeti loomed over her with eyes of a predator. He crouched down and grabbed her with two hands and ten jagged claws, and slung her over his shoulder. She tried to wriggle free from over his shoulder, but he dug his claws into her flesh and jailed the prisoner within his grasp. It was no use to struggle. It just made the claws sink deeper.

"Bigfoot!...no.." She whimpered with her hand reaching towards the cliff. She lost hope in him hearing her and watched forlornly as they ascended the steep mountain. The yeti clung to rocks and ragged earth as the air grew thin and cooler, much like Betty's heart. *Is he dead? What will become of me?*

Betty nestled her hands deep into the thick, musty fur of the yeti. The air was brisk and frost was on the ground. The sun was still high in the sky, but provided no heat because of the thinning air. Her body began shivering with fear and cold. The yeti much preferred a wintery climate and such trips down the mountain were as short as possible for he could not stand the heat and warm sun.

Through crunching snow and pine trees he marched tirelessly. She was sure her cheeks and nose were bright red from the wind and her fingers and toes yellow and bloodless. A lone tear ran down her cheek. Surely, she would not make it in these conditions. Surely, she would be food and not his friend or mate. Surely, she would never see her Bigfoot again.

They made it to the top of the mountain and were welcomed by millions of tiny prisms scattered across the craggy peak. The sun beams glistened inside every molecule of perfectly white snow. Betty was sure she had never seen anything more beautiful. Though, when one looked closely, one would realize the entire site was littered with bones. As if all he did was sit on his mountain and kill. *This is a graveyard - he mustn't have smelled my berries.* She wondered how the yeti knew she was there.

Betty landed in a deep pile of powdered crystal as the yeti relieved himself next to her. She was frozen to the core as her satin robe proved useless and shamefully hoped his urine would trickle in her direction and offer temporary warmth. She pulled her legs and arms into herself and curled up into a helpless little ball of Betty. Unfortunately, her current position with her knees crossed over her chest enabled the yeti to see her satin underwear - and the impression her vaginal mounds made on it. He crouched down and hooked his index finger into the crotch of her panties and ripped them clean off. The cold air tickled her vagina and made her shudder. The yeti stood erect and glared down at her powerless body and his hanging cock began to grow. Even though he was taller and wider than Bigfoot, his little soldier was not. It reminded Betty of a white worm - or an albino snake. Roughly a foot long and as wide as a carrot, it hung crookedly to the left while blue and purple veins pulsed throughout its shaft. It was one unappetizing cock. Lucky for Betty - and her life - she wasn't one to quit and she would take this one for the team if it meant she could see Bigfoot again. She wasn't ready to die, and, in which life would one have the opportunity to fuck Bigfoot AND a yeti? She hoped his body would keep her warm. She anticipated his thick, fluffy groin hair as he crawled up on top of her, holding his weight upon his knuckles like a gorilla; his long, skinny cock padded against her vagina like a loose shutter in the wind. She looked up into his haggard face and pondered his leathery, wrinkled skin. *How old is this beast?* The yeti reminder her of her haggard old neighbor, Mr. Calhoun. That pervert was always spying on Betty through his window with a pair of binoculars. *Maybe if I satisfy this dirty old man, he'll fall asleep and I can flee to Bigfoot!*

The old leathery cock brushed against her vagina, bouncing and rolling against its tender flesh each time he adjusted himself. Still frigidly cold she couldn't move; he grabbed her legs and raised her buttocks off the ground and up into the air, his large strong hands wrapped around her lower legs, his cock was long, but not strong and thick like Bigfoot's and it couldn't hold up the weight of its bulbous tip. He held both legs in his left hand, like a hunter with his kill, and supported his wobbling cock with his right. The yeti directed the purple fleshy tip towards her vagina, clumsily pushing at the entrance. Her clam was scared shut and wouldn't allow his wiggling white worm to penetrate her. The sensation of pressing his tip against her pussy was sending tiny electric bolts throughout his leathery old ballsack; precum began seeping out of his urethra and lubricating Betty's mounds. Her sealed clam became slippery and gave way to his bulbous purple tip to slip between her lips.

"Arhuuhhhhh…." He moaned.

The giant, hairy yeti thrust his needy old cock in and out his tiny prisoner's warm, tight pussy. Betty was amazed at the yetis competence and dexterity, for she was sure he would be a fumbling, bumbling mess, just as Bigfoot was. *Is it possible the yeti once had a lover?* He pushed and fed his skinny cock deeper into her slippery pussy moaning and grunting; for Betty, it was a strange sensation - a thin, veiny shaft with such a large, bulbous, fleshy tip. His hot, purple glans thrust deeper and deeper-

"Arhuugh! Hrrmf...Hrrmf.." He was grunting guttural,

ugly noises as his claws dug into her calves. Suddenly, Betty heard a crunching sound in the distance: snow and bones splintering and crumbling getting louder. The yeti didn't react, for he was in ecstasy and his tiny brain was lost in lust.

"Arhuugh!...Arhu-uu-u.." The yeti convulsed and came rapidly with each contraction. Deep within her pussy she felt his large glans pulsating and throbbing as it spew out hot cum deep into her crevices; the warm sperm oozed from her pussy when -

CRACK. The yetis eyes crossed as he fell to the side with a thump. His thick, foamy tongue lolled out of his mouth and melted the snow around it; his flaccid penis retreated beneath its foreskin for protection from the cold. Bigfoot stood valiantly above her as the setting sun formed a glowing halo around his head and highlighted the large animal's thigh bone he grasped in his hand.

Chapter 7: Home

Bigfoot snarled when he saw Betty's dripping pussy. He lifted her her up and flung her over the yeti's unconscious body. He tore open Betty's robe and flared his nostrils, snorting and puffing with adrenaline and exertion from his hasty climb to win back his maiden. Bigfoot's cock engorged as he watched her breasts tickle with chills and goosebumps, her nipples erect from excitement. Bigfoot studied her delicate waist, tiny belly button and soft, hairless skin all covered in tiny goosebumps. She stared into his dark, ominous eyes that were now fervent and animalistic, she saw his desire, his *need* - and she needed him. Betty grabbed underneath her thighs and spread her legs wide; Bigfoot grabbed his gigantic, thick shaft and stroked the throbbing veins. He worked his grapefruit sized globe-of-a-glans up and down her pussy lips, massaging them. His gnarled, beastly hand grabbing at her breasts, clawing and manhandling the large mounds of fresh flesh. He shoved a calloused, hairy middle finger into her pussy, the black tufts of wiry hair glistened from her pussy juice. He tasted her.

"Grrr…" A low, beastly growl escaped his throat. She tasted better than pie.

Grunting and snorting he pushed and shoved his enormous one-eyed-monster into her; his grapefruit glans breaking way into the slippery hot and fleshy hole be desired. *Bigfoot take back Bigfoot's slave! Bigfoot own human!*

Betty reveled in the naughtiness of it all, for she was raised a hard Catholic and had only made love to one man before and had only even kissed one man before. She knew now that she never loved Brad. *This* was her new life and this life would be an adventure! She relished the risqué, she desired the dirty and was titillated by the taboo of being owned and fucked by this huge beast who ruled nature and could knock down trees with his gigantic cock.

Betty's fragile little fingers palpated her soft, voluptuous breasts, squeezing and pushing them together while fingering her nipples; Bigfoot's huge cock thrusted into her, rubbing her back against the thick warm hair of the yeti. She was being taken atop the highest peak of the forest on a snow capped mountain and laughed about the life she left below. Betty's world spun in delight and ecstasy and knew now where she was meant to be; a tear rolled down her cheek as she appreciated the absurdity of it all. Squeezing her breasts and moaning, smiling, her pussy grew warmer and thicker as blood pumped into its flesh; the sensations rising, she felt herself climb the mountain of ecstasy. Bigfoot's cock couldn't fit more than halfway inside of her, it was far too long, but she accompanied the girth and stretched as far as she possibly could, the walls of her pussy stinging. The entirety of her cavity was tingling with hot pinpricks as he rubbed inside her, against her anus and g-spot, her bladder forcefully emptied; the long wiry hairs on his veiny shaft tickled her clitoris and lips, it was a wild sensation, which hurled her over the edge:

"Oh, Bigfoot! Oh, Bigfoot! Oh, give it to me; fuck me with your monster cock!"

The sound of her dainty feminine voice littered with expletives tickled his ears as his keen nose picked up the scent of the pleasure juices squirting from her pussy. He grabbed both of her thighs and rammed himself into her, squashing his thick fleshy glans against the raw walls of her vagina:

"Holy shit, fuck me, fuck me! This is so wild! Fuck me, Bigfoot, shoot your monster load inside me!"

His testicles danced with each jolt of lighting as they contracted and spewed out loads and loads of steaming cum into her; fluids gushed out from her pussy as his cock inhabited the entire volume. Pussy juice, urine and viscous cum soaked the yeti underneath her. Her tiny pussy stung from the salty cum.

Bigfoot's softening cock pulsates within her. She smiled dreamily and stroked his thick arm hair. She gazed lovingly into Bigfoot's emotionless, dark eyes.

The yeti began to stir, he was awakening from the hard blow. Betty slid down off her furry warm bed and backed away; Bigfoot stood up strong and mighty. The yeti, shaking cobwebs from his head, was bewildered as his eyes came into focus. He howled:

"*Arrrhhhuuughhhh*!" Birds flew out from their nests into the safe sky as he snarled at Bigfoot with fury, his fists clenched.

"*Hrr-grrrrmm*!" he snarled back in defense, shielding Betty away with a long, muscular arm.

"*Arrrr-HUUUUGGGH!*" The yeti beat his chest and roared into the sky.

"*Grumpf-Grumpf. Hrr-grumpf.*" Bigfoot's tone changed - it sounded like he had an idea.

This time the yeti did not reply. Betty peered over Bigfoot's shielding arm and saw a sad expression in the beast's face.

Bigfoot slung his mate over his shoulder and kept a giant hand on her back to keep her warm as they descended the snowy mountain. Betty was filled with delight to know that was finally over and now it would only be she and Bigfoot to rule the forest together. Her mind overflowed with plans to make their home cozy and livable, from fur pelts and hand made mattresses, carved wood cutlery and - *oh, golly!* - a fire pit!

"Perhaps, if we find a goat we can use its milk and make cheese. Then we can make a pizza - oh I *love* pizza!" Bigfoot didn't like how chatty Betty had become.

"*Grumpf.*" He grunted shortly and gave her a shake, hoping to shut her up.

"...Yes, don't you worry! New ways to make love, too. Ah, men, always thinking with the other head…" Betty was over the moon as the moonlight itself danced upon the forest treetops. She was too busy fantasizing to notice Bigfoot had carried her all the way back to where the big oak trees met her lush, green lawn.

Betty's dreamy eyes shot open when she recognized her pretty white house.

"Hey!" She beat a tiny first on the beast's solid back,

"Why are we here?!"

Bigfoot did not answer the female human.

"*Hey*! Answer me! Don't you bring me home! No, sir - don't you dare!" With furious fists and wild legs she pleaded, "damn you! I am not just a sex toy!"

Bigfoot dropped betty onto the soft blades of grass. Betty, with tears in her eyes looked up at Bigfoot and dug her tiny fingers into his fur. But he wasn't looking at her. He was looking out into calm of the picket fence community. He raised his furry hand and uncurled a giant, calloused finger, and pointed.

"Mrs. Merryweather?" Betty asked.

BONUS STORY!

Pounded by the Garden Gnome

A Big Toe-Sucking Good Time

By Eva Roche-Poésy

Chapter One: Sadie's Fetish

Some say it's a strange thing to sexualize one's feet.
Especially a garden gnome's.

But there exists a story of a young lady who, at the age of 32, was not quite sure when her fascination began, but it had certainly led her on a long and curious journey. It's not easy to find a real gnome. For one, they're not keen on today's technology. You won't find one on Tinder. So where do you find one? And how do you know if he's keen on foot worship?

Well let's think for a moment. What's one thing a gnome loves more than a good full pipe and his mum?
Gardening!

Like the lovers of the earth and luscious soil, Sadie took

to her nearest Home Depot. She stalked the aisles for a few days and her efforts turned up empty. But then it dawned on her: what self respecting gnome would subject themselves to the obscene florescent lighting and heavy chemical smells that plague the enormous warehouse chains? She quickly googled all the well established mom and pop gardening shops and whittled the results down to the few who have been around the longest. Her heart began racing as she read aloud the address of the shop which had remained:

Gran and Dildo Gnomby

Tilled Earth

140 Rolling Hill Way

Wiltfordshire PA, 15069

Sadie spritzed herself with her favorite perfume and hopped in her hooptie. She turned on her favorite jam -

some Michael Bublé - and put the pedal to the medal. Two Starbucks' iced soy lattes and one urine-filled plastic cup later, she had arrived at her destination! Oh, how she squirmed with anticipation.

With one foot in front of the other, she followed the meticulously groomed pathway, for nary a weed was to be found nor a stone out of place, and began to smell a rather peculiar scent. It was a sweet smell, warm with cinnamon and fresh with citrus. Surrounded by luscious trees bearing fruits and flowers bowing to her presence, she had a really good feeling about what may come.

At the end of the pathway stood the entrance to the peculiar home business. It was a large, heavy wooden door made of thick cherry wood planks and each generously oiled. A few inches above the large brass door knob hung a hand made copper sign, which read:

Gran & Son

prized bushes

second to none'

Sadie pursed her lips. She was sure the sign meant that their pruning skills were top notch, but she couldn't help but wonder. Alas, she rapped her knuckles upon the door and listened intently for any movement inside. The large door creaked open and a little, very little old lady, whose pointy red hat stood as high as Sadie's knee, greeted her. "Hello, good morning! Good morning to you!" She said. "Oh, hello! I'm sorry to bother you but what is that delicious smell? I was just driving by but could smell it all the way down the road." She replied.

"Oh, my dear, just a few cakes now, just a few cakes! Come in, please do, very busy now. I'm very busy here, but please do come in." The old lady shuffled back inside and began hanging tea towels.

"Good morning, dear, please be welcome," she had a high, crackling voice but somehow stayed quite pleasant to Sadie's ear. "Would you care for some tea, dear? Some tea perhaps. And a cake, yes? Oh, we've got such lovely cake."

"Oh, yes, thank you very much." Sadie was pleased with the woman's hospitality.

"Dildo!" The woman yelled. Sadie's eyes shot open, for what on earth would an old lady be yelling out dildo for -- and in front of a stranger? "Dildo, dear!"

"Yes, mum," came a low voice from somewhere deeper inside the tunneled home. Dildo, Sadie wondered, surely that's not the poor guy's name, right?

"Dildo, dear, we have a visitor. Fetch the girl some cake and I'll put the kettle on."

"Yes, mum."

The poor little man, she thought.

The gnomes were magnificent bakers. Cakes and pies from lemon loaves to blueberry cobbler and cinnamon swirled breads. It was surely a delicious morning, but that wasn't the only thing that whetted Sadie's mouth. Dildo's bare feet had been tempting her all the while. They were impressively clean and well cared for, impressively large for belonging to a man the size of a little lawn ornament and excitingly animated: his toes wiggled gleefully with each bite of cake Dildo took. The two went on chattering about what a lovely morning it was while Sadie squirmed in her seat. What long, suckable toes he has!

"Hello, dear?" A high voice started to break through Sadie's deep thoughts. "Dear are you alright? Have you had enough cake perhaps?"

"Oh, I'm so sorry." She apologized for her mental

absence. "Maybe I did have too much sugar."

"Well best idea then, I say, best is to walk it off in the lovely garden, then. Very good idea. Fresh air for ye will only do good!" Gran tugged gently at Sadie's pant leg and urged her out the door. It's quite possible she was afraid the young girl may let out some dreadful odor and muddle the scents of her fresh baked goods. "You too, Dildo. You make sure now the young dear doesn't get lost amongst the shrubbery." A curious woman she certainly is, for only someone the height of a gnome would get lost there.

Dildo did not excel at small talk and therefore kept himself busy within the garden, but remained nearby the human, lest she get into trouble or step on his turnips. But she did not wander away, for it was him she was there for.

"So, you like gardening?" She asked.

"Right so, indeed." He answered, inspecting his tools.

"I've got a basil plant at home. Well, I didn't grow it myself, but it's in a pot…" Dildo thrust the handle of a garden hoe into her hand, cutting off her dreadful idea of small talk. She inspected the hoe, which was impressively clean, and thus quipped, "a dirty hoe is a happy hoe!"

He raised an eyebrow and responded, "My dear, hoes don't have feelings, they're merely tools."

Dildo began pumping a small lever that stood out of the ground and unwound the hose from its stand, but when he opened the tap, no water gave way. "For this is the kinkiest hose I've ever had the displeasure of dealing with! Darn cheap garden hose!" He grumbled as he twist and turned the crumpled rubber.

"I'm kinkier than a cheap garden hose," I snickered, running my hand up and down the hoe's wooden handle. Dildo didn't catch on, but pursed his lips and mumbled under his breath, "Humans! They really are dumber than dogwart."

As her delicious little morsel of a man struggled with the kinky hose, she noticed a few drops of water had escaped from the nozzle. An immediate rush of warmth filled her vagina. The lone droplets had wetted his perfectly groomed and brushed foot hair, matting it slightly to its thick, yet smooth skin.

She got down faster than a horny snowman in the Sahara desert, and focused intently on the beautiful sight before her. Sadie couldn't hold back any longer. She couldn't hold up the charade of actually enjoying gardening! What she wanted to enjoy was this little man's enormous, thick-soled feet and hairy toes wiggling inside of her mouth!

Her hands wrapped around his bony ankles and felt the twists and turns of his dark leg hair. They seemed to beckon her down and guide her towards his toes; the hair growing softer, yet thicker. The hair which grew on his feet sat like a beloved bush, a luscious plant that grew from the most richest earth; a mound of pubic hair from a 70s porno flick carefully grafted to a 3-foot tall man's 2-foot wide massive stomping feet. She nestled her nose into the shocked gnome's foot-bush and inhaled deeply. This is for what her life was meant!

"Excuse me? Excuse me, miss, did you drop something?" Dildo stammered and tried his best to hide the bewilderment which rattled him. What woman in her best mind should be, or would want to be, smelling a gnomes foot?!

"Oh, Dildo!" Sadie gasped between breaths, "it's your feet!" Equally confused and terrified, Dildo took a step backward, because, surely this woman had lost her mind.

Sadie's primal urge refused to allow her life's calling to escape her grip. Taking hold of his clean, pressed leather shorts (quite similar in appearance to lederhosen) she pulled the creature closer to her. She was on her knees, yet with his small stature it meant they were now eye to eye. Mouth to mouth.

With dear old gran peeking out from the window, she wrapped her large humanoid arm behind the little man's head and brought him to her wanting mouth. Enveloping his face within hers, she darted her eager tongue into his nervous yet kind mouth. He did not fight back, for he was only genuinely courteous and kind. She licked his teeth and tasted the remnants of lemon cake dusted with cinnamon. Drawing her tongue up the side of his close-shaven cheek until his sideburns tickled her lips, the gnome's walls began to crumble. "Ohh," a low moan escaped his tight mouth. His lusciously brown curling locks twirled effortlessly around her fingers. Sadie was intoxicated by this little man, but now she needed to know if what they say is true about men with big feet... *Does he have a big monsterous dick?!*

To his granny's horror she pressed her body against his. Their scents mingled within the magical little gnome garden his gran and him worked so hard on throughout the years. She felt her gaze fixed upon them, but she knew in the back of her mind, that Gran was feeling equally horrified with witnessing her only grandson being downright molested by such a horny human, and as mesmerized as a second-generation Italian boy watching a Yankee game, the moment A-Rod calls off his retirement and steps back onto the field, thus dropping the mic for all of baseball eternity...

Dildo was in shock, to say the least. What human, what female human would do such a thing?! There must be hundreds, thousands of well proportioned human men out there falling over themselves for the slightest chance of squeezing just one of Sadie's squishy, perfect breasts. (Sadie didn't know it, but gnomes loved breasts, and lucky for her she was blessed with an extra squishy set of 34DD; her pearly white skin had hypnotized him from the beginning!) As her extra large fun bags (which were actually larger than his head) rubbed and pressed themselves against his anxious and deprived body, he felt his member grow. Since Dildo had quite a small figure, Sadie felt the new presence immediately. And yes, now we know what they say about men with big feet!

Gran-gran rooted on as she watched her only grandson and sole heir to the business become enveloped in pure ecstasy. Sadie knew it was now or never, despite being amongst the innocent plants, despite being watched by his gran, despite being in plain sight where any garden-fancy lad or lass may meander... She tipped the straps of his suspenders over his shoulders; the weight of his leather shorts pulled themselves off his body and onto the earth with a thud. Dildo's jaw dropped as he stood in disbelief. Never had he dreamt of a human female being remotely interested in him, nevertheless one taking him over! He watched as the silky blond head made way south, kissing and nuzzling the flesh and hair that peered out from between the buttons of his flannel shirt, which she carefully unbuttoned one by one.

Sadie's senses buzzed as she inhaled his masculine scent. He smelled of musky, oiled wood, ancient spices and the faintest hint of sweat. She worked diligently at the tiny pearl buttons of his hand printed, woven flannel shirt. Pushing her nose throughout his chest hair and working her fingers through the curls she exercised the tufts and burls as if to say, "you are fetterless; be free!"

Dildo grunted and squirmed as Sadie found knots within the forest of his chest. He watched helplessly as she made her way south to his growing member; her generous tits giving warmth and comfort as they rested on his tent below. "S-Sadie-" Dildo began, "There are still kinks in my hose I need to--"

"I've got enough kinks for you," Sadie breathed into the thick curling forest that circled his belly button, "forget the hose!" Her trembling hands shot up his muscular, stocky legs and rested upon the two quivering mounds behind him. His member pulsated behind the hand stitched knickers his old gran made for him. Throb, throb, throb, Sadie yearned for his undoubtedly virgin manhood.

The thick hair curled out from the knickers as she ventured south towards his nether region. The twirls of hair grabbed at her eyelashes; the silken ends teased her nostrils. The mound meant for a giant pushed eagerly against her throat.

"Your dick is growing like a weed!" She exclaimed, genuinely impressed.

"Please pardon me, I must take off my knickers before they rip at the seams." Dildo was awfully worried about ruining his hand made undies, but Sadie took the task upon herself and before he knew it, they had been flung through the air, landing upon the brass door knob.

And there it hung. Slightly to the left, but ultimately a straight pointer with a nicely tanned color, Dildo Gnomby erect, majestic gnome dick saluted Sadie with a keen and thoughtful eye. It stood proudly at a good 12-inches and along with its girth, undoubtedly not for the faint of heart. She cupped his gnome balls and struggled to fit the tip of his engorged member into her mouth. She slobbered his knob up and down and all around and worked her hands on his shaft, her fingers rippling over bulging veins. Dildo moaned and grunted and swirled into a cloud of ecstasy. He had never received head before, that is certain, but what's more peculiar is that he had never even successfully masterbated. So much blood had left his brain in efforts to fill his giant penis, that he swiftly became light headed and fell backwards into a pile of good tilled earth.

Dildo awoke to Sadie's kind face and blonde hair shining with the sun behind her. Her generous breasts heaved upon his chest. "Oh, oh good morning," Dildo began, "sorry I had bit of a--"

Sadie pulled the top of her shirt down and let her tits spill out. She massaged them on either side of his head as he blushed hard and his eyes rolled in opposite directions. He was slightly suffocating, but in the most loveliest of ways, so that made almost dying OK.

Dildo's dick began poking and jabbing at Sadie's stomach, eager for more attention. But what's a girl love more than a gnome's enormous dick? His hairy feet! Oh, the glorious hair. Sadie caressed her fair skin along his plushy foot hair and smiled. She kissed each toe and licked each tuft of hair that sat upon them. Sucking hard, sucking gently; she caressed the high arches of his feet, nibbling at every curve and crevice. His feet smelled like earth. They smelled of life and long travels, of hard work and masculinity. No human man, no matter how tall, could have feet as large and noble as Dildo's. She worshipped the skilled feet with her hands, her eyes, nose and mouth, but it wasn't enough for her.

"Take my breasts with your feet, Dildo!" She growled at him lowly, "take them and squeeze them with your toes!" Dildo did as ordered and worked her large breasts with his large feet and squished and squeezed their flesh between his toes like wet sand. "Oh, Dildo, your feet are so sexy!" Dildo began to wonder if all female humans were so strange and attracted to feet, when Sadie really threw him through a loop. "Fuck me, Dildo, fuck me with your feet."

Sadie laid back onto the gnomes' prized soil and spread

her legs. Lifting her skirt, she revealed no underwear. Dildo stared between her legs, her hairless legs, and into a slightly agape peach-colored pussy. The hairless fruit beckoned him as he inched a timid toe towards its beauty. He rubbed his big toe against her slit; each movement making the peach grow more moist. Sadie ached for him. Dildo slipped his big hairy toe deep into her vagina and moaned at the warmth, which traveled all the way up his body. "Oh, Dildo!" Sadie exclaimed, "more! I want more of your big hairy foot inside of me!"

Dildo toe fucked her as he stroked his enormous member. He watched his toe enter and exit the ripest peach he had ever seen. Sadie rubbed her breasts and moaned, twirling in delight and ecstasy. Dildo, the ever so nimble gnome, had perched himself above her without missing a toe-fucking beat and replaced his foot with his throbbing dick. He wanted to feel what a smooth and beautiful female human felt like. He worked his engorged tip into her wet pussy and shivered at the sudden warmth. He thrust himself in, but only managed to enter a few inches. Sadie adjusted herself and opened her hips wider to accept him. Dildo worked his cock deeper and deeper into her delicious flesh; feeling her from all angles and watched as her giant breasts jiggled and heaved. "Oh, Dildo, oh, Dildo!" Sadie moaned as she became dangerously close to the land of no return. Beads of sweat from the midday sun fell from his face and tickled her tits. Dildo was working harder now than he ever did in the garden, for it took much power and concentration to work such a huge appendage when you're such a tiny person. Alas, his testicles tingled and shot signals up to his brain and down his thickening shaft; the tip of his cock became bulbous and full of tiny lightning bolts, throbbing all at once, but when he saw Sadie's eyes roll back he, too, was not going to return. Dildo's testicles shot into his body as an undulating movement took over his enormous shaft; globs and globs of kept sperm were making their way towards the glorious exit.

"Dildo, oh my God, fuck me, fuck me you little garden gnome!" The walls of her pussy locked down like a giant fist around his trapped member and throbbed rhythmically, her engorged clit danced and pulsated from the teasing of the thick curls of gnome pubic hair. "I'm coming, Dildo, oh fuck me I'm coming!" Sadie screamed out for all the world to hear. Dildo met her screams with grunts and moans as the globs of sperm became forceful spits of hot cum splattering inside her; his thrusts became spastic helpless jerks as the last of his hot viscous cum escaped him.

Granny looked on as the two new interracial love birds panted and gasped for breath. It was a bittersweet moment for dear gran, as she came to realize she had just lost her beloved grandson to a human, but that he had also finally got his rocks off. She used to worry about him, but now she'll only have to worry about a halfling running through the garden.

And knitting a new pair of knickers.

***

<u>That's the end of the bundle!</u>

If I helped to heat up your day and put a smile on your face then I would love to hear from you. You can write me directly at <u>evarpoesy@gmail.com</u> or join my mailing list from my Author's page.

From sizzling specials to sexy sneak previews, Eva's books will keep you wanting more - and your (in)box will thank you.